"There are spies every-where!" Mary Jo whispered. "I overheard some kids from Mrs. O'Hara's class talking. I think they're going to try and find out how we're decorating our snowman."

Just listening to them talk about the Winter Carnival snowman problems made me feel lonely in a funny kind of way. Everybody was being very nice to me. But they were on the snowman team, having all these problems together, and I wasn't. . . .

Elspeth Campbell Murphy

CURTIS ANDERSON

Illustrated by Tony Kenyon

Chariot Books
DAVID C. COOK PUBLISHING CO.

A Wise Owl Book
Published by Chariot Books, an imprint of David C. Cook Publishing Co.
David C. Cook Publishing Co., Elgin, Illinois 60120
David C. Cook Publishing Co., Weston, Ontario

CURTIS ANDERSON
© 1986 by Elspeth Campbell Murphy

Illustrated by Tony Kenyon
Cover and book design by Catherine Hesz Colten

Printed in the United States of America
90 89 88   2 3 4 5

Library of Congress Cataloging-in-Publication Data

Murphy, Elspeth Campbell.
  Curtis Anderson.

  (The Kids from Apple Street Church ; 6)
  "A Wise owl book."
  Summary: In his prayer journal, Curtis Anderson records how he allows the other kids to jump to a wrong conclusion about how he broke his leg, even though the truth would help his crusade to convince them that he is just as ordinary as they are.
  [1. Fractures—Fiction. 2. Self-perception—Fiction. 3. Christian life—Fiction. 4. Diaries] I. Kenyon, Tony, ill. II. Title. III. Series.
PZ7.M95316Cu   1986   [Fic.]   86-8819
ISBN 1-55513-027-5

"First Snow" from A POCKETFUL OF POEMS by Marie Louise Allen.
Copyright, 1939, by Harper & Row Publishers, Inc. Copyright © 1957 by Mary Allen Howarth.
Reprinted by permission of Harper & Row Publishers, Inc.

*To my husband, Michael,
and the many kids he has taught over the years
who remind us of Curtis, Danny, and Pug,
Mary Jo, Julie, and Becky*

Thursday

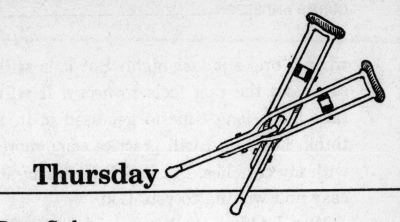

Dear God,

This is a good time to write in my prayer journal. That's because I have to sit here quietly with my leg propped up.

Outside the snow is coming down in those nice, big, fat flakes. They're my favorite kind. I don't like skimpy, little snowflakes that much.

It's kind of cozy sitting on the couch with a pillow and comforter. I practiced my guitar for a while. Usually I have school, but I have to stay home for a couple of days. It's good just to sit here for a change.

My leg doesn't hurt as much as it did

when I broke it last night. But it is still sore, and the cast feels *so heavy*! It will take me a long time to get used to it, I think. Later on I will practice some more with my crutches. But now I am taking it easy and writing to you, God.

Miss Jenkins, our Sunday school teacher, gave each of us a notebook to use for a prayer journal. She said it would be like writing a PRIVATE letter to you and that we could tell you anything we want.

So it is not great to have a broken leg, God, but it isn't all bad either. The really bad part is thinking about HOW I broke it. When I think about that, I feel REALLY STUPID. And feeling stupid is just about one of the worst feelings there is.

You are the only one besides me who knows *exactly what happened,* God. I'm glad you already know everything, because I don't feel like writing it down in my journal. I know my journal is *private,* but I just don't want to see the dumb thing I did all written down in words on the paper.

My parents and my sister, Claudia, know *where* I fell: *in the bathroom.* But even they don't know *how* it happened.

I don't want anyone else to know even the bathroom part!

Claudia and I were home alone last night, because my parents were at a meeting and my brother, Coby, was back at college after vacation.

According to Claudia, she was baby-sitting for me. But I told her I didn't need a teenage sister baby-sitter and that we just happened to be in the house at the same time, that's all.

But Claudia says, "Ha! You'd just better

be glad I was there, Curtis James!"

What can I say? She's right about that.

Last night when I hurt myself (and I'm not telling ANYBODY about the goofy way it happened), Claudia called my parents at their meeting. Only, they weren't there yet. So Claudia left a message for them to meet us at the hospital. Then Claudia drove me in our other car to the emergency room.

She hasn't had her driver's license very long, so I think she had a pretty good time doing that. In fact, I think she'll drive around all the time now, looking for people who hurt themselves—so she can take them to the hospital!

Don't get me wrong, God. I mean, it was pretty good thinking for Claudia to take me to the emergency room. But every time she talks about her part in the story it gets bigger and bigger. Do you know what I mean? So now it's like: *Curtis's Broken Leg. The Movie. Starring—CLAUDIA ANDERSON!!!*

I don't want Mrs. Whitney, my teacher, or Miss Jenkins, my Sunday school teacher, or Pastor Bennett or any of the kids to find out where I was when I broke my leg. So I made my parents and Claudia promise not to tell. And they said OK. Who knows? Maybe they are a little bit embarrassed, too. Maybe they think it is pretty goofy to fall down and break your leg *in the bathroom.*

You know my family, God. My brother, Coby, gets straight A's in college. My sister, Claudia, gets straight A's in high school. My father is a high school principal. And my mother teaches in a business school. They are all nice, but not one of

11

them is the least little bit goofy. And I don't know what they would think if they knew this secret: SOMEONE in your family is goofy. (So, if you don't tell, God, I sure won't!)

● ● ●

I think I must have fallen asleep for a while, because the next time I looked at the clock, I saw it was time for school to be out.

Then I looked out the window, and I saw Pug McConnell and Danny Petrowski coming toward my house. They are both in my class, so I figured maybe Mrs. Whitney gave them some work for me to do.

The first thing Pug said to me when he got here was, "Wow, are you lucky! It's too bad you got your leg broken, but at least you got to play ice hockey with those teenagers!"

"Yeah!" said Danny. "They don't usually let younger kids play with them. I would have been too scared, though! Ice hockey goes so fast! And the players get in fights a lot, right?"

Then Pug asked, "Did your leg get broken in a fight? Or did you just turn around too fast on the ice and fall down?"

Pug and Danny were talking so fast, God, it took me awhile to understand what they were talking about. And then it hit me! They thought I broke my leg *playing ice hockey with teenagers*!

"Wait a minute!" I said. "Did *Mrs. Whitney* say that about ice hockey?"

"No," said Danny. "Mrs. Whitney just told the class you broke your leg."

Pug said, "But at recess some kids said you were playing ice hockey with teenagers."

13

"THAT'S CRAZY!" I said. "Why would teenagers let *me* play with them?"

"Why not?" said Pug. "Coby used to play with you, didn't he? I wish I had an older brother instead of all sisters! One *little* sister is enough! Why did I have to get four *older* ones, too?

I knew what Pug was talking about, God. *One* Claudia is bad enough!

But I said, "Coby used to play with me sometimes when it was just him and me. But he would *never* let me be on a team with him and his friends. Not in a million years!"

Pug and Danny thought about that for a minute. Then they just said, "Oh."

They sounded so disappointed I felt sorry for them. But then I thought to myself, Hey, wait a minute! *I'm* the one with the broken leg. And I didn't break it in a fun,

neat way—like playing ice hockey. I broke it in a dumb, stupid way.

"So how *did* you break your leg?" asked Danny.

"I just . . . fell, that's all," I said. And then I knew I had to change the subject. FAST.

"Hey, you two can be the first people to sign my cast besides my parents and Claudia," I said. They liked that.

15

And then I asked if they brought me the work from today. They got it out and explained what I was supposed to do. It didn't look too bad.

It stopped snowing, and Pug and Danny had to leave. They wanted to earn some money by shoveling people's sidewalks. I wished I could go with them. I'm not crazy about shoveling walks, but I thought it would be OK if you got paid by people. And it would even be fun if you could do the work with a friend.

● ● ●

I figured Becky Garcia would come over with my reading work, and I was right.

Becky and I go to the next grade for reading, and we are in the same group. It feels kind of funny being with older kids, because you always wonder if they think you're too twirpy to be with them. And

16

there's *a lot* of work, God! Sometimes I wish the group didn't have to go so fast, but that's just how Mrs. Jones is.

Becky and I don't like Mrs. Jones, our reading teacher, as much as we like Mrs. Whitney, our regular teacher. That's because Mrs. Jones is super-super-SUPER-strict. Everything has to be exactly right, and if you don't get your work done— WATCH OUT!

Mrs. Whitney makes us do our work, too, but she's not as mean about it as Mrs. Jones is.

Becky said, "Mrs. Jones had a substitute today, and some of the kids were really bad. So I bet Mrs. Jones yells at everyone when she gets back—even the kids who didn't do anything."

Becky shivered just thinking about it. She hates getting yelled at. I knew what she meant. "Mrs. Jones really scares me," I said.

Becky stared at me with her mouth open wide. Finally she said, "You're kidding! I thought *I* was the only one who was scared to go to reading! I didn't think you were scared of anything—especially not after the way you broke your leg!"

"I *wasn't* playing ice hockey with teenagers!" I almost yelled.

Becky looked at me like she didn't have any idea what I was talking about.

"I know," she said. "You didn't break your leg *playing* on the ice. You *slipped on the ice* when you saved that little kid who ran in front of the truck. You grabbed him just in the nick of time. But you fell and broke your leg. Right? That's what some of the kids at school said."

Good grief! That story was even crazier

than the story Pug and Danny heard!

I said, "No, Becky. That's *not* what happened! I just . . . fell, that's all."

"How?" she asked.

"Oh, it was just—nothing. How's your puppy?"

I thought that would be a good way to change the subject. And it worked!

Becky has a new puppy named No-el. That might seem like a funny name for a dog, except that she got him for Christmas.

Becky couldn't stay long, because she had to go walk No-el and the other dogs on her dog-walking job.

Before she left, she lent me a book she had just finished reading. She said, "This is the neatest book! You don't find out until the very last chapter that the nice old lady who lives next door is really an enemy spy."

19

"Becky!" I said. "You just gave away the ending!"

Becky clapped her hand over her mouth like she couldn't believe what a dumb thing she just did.

I didn't want her to feel dumb, God, because that is a *bad* feeling. I know. So I said, "Never mind. If you think it's a good book, I'll read it anyway."

I think that made her feel better. And then I told her she could sign my cast just like Pug and Danny did. She said her brother, Bobby, would probably want to sign it himself when he saw me. But she signed No-el's name for him.

After Becky left, I started reading the book. I always like to know before I start a new book that someone else thought it was really good.

Someday maybe I'll write books for other people to read. Right now I just write stories for myself.

I know Becky writes stories, because she let me read a couple of them. I thought they were very good. But I haven't showed my stories to anyone, because what I wrote might seem too wild and goofy. I sort of have my own kind of science fiction and adventure stories. Mostly I like to write about this boy called Jamie. I named him that because my middle name is James. But Jamie sounds better in the story.

● ● ●

Reading the mystery book helped me not to think about things for a while. But then at supper I got to thinking about what Becky had said about me saving a little kid from getting run over by a truck.

It really bothered me, God, in a funny kind of way. I mean, I always thought it

21

would bother me a lot if kids said *bad* things about me that weren't true. But I found out it's also embarrassing if people say *good* things that aren't true.

Why did people think I would do something that brave? I don't think I'm brave at all. And I don't think people know me very well, if they think I'm brave.

After supper I did my regular schoolwork and started my reading work. But I didn't get to finish it right away because I got *more visitors*. (I think I had more visitors today than I ever had in my whole life!)

Pastor Bennett came by to visit. He visits all the sick people from Apple Street Church. I'm not sick-sick. I feel OK, and I'm learning to get around pretty well. But I was still glad he came.

His daughter, Mary Jo, came with him,

since she is in my Sunday school class and my regular class, too.

On the way they stopped to pick up Julie Chang. And Julie's kindergarten sister, Amy, wanted to come, too.

So they all came in to see me.

Mary Jo never exactly walks. She sort of bounces when she's indoors. And she runs when she's outdoors. She always wants to race me, because she sort of beat me once or twice. But that was an accident.

Anyway, Mary Jo came in so bouncy that she tripped on the coffee table. She almost fell on my cast, but she caught herself just in time and landed with a thud on the edge of the chair.

"Mary Jo, settle down," her father said.

Then he talked to me in that funny-serious voice he sometimes uses when he's kidding around. He said, "I don't usually take Mary Jo with me to visit the sick, because we've found it takes them twice as long to get better if I do. But since you're a special friend, we thought you might want someone to come over and jump on your cast."

"Oh, Daddy!" said Mary Jo. Then she turned to me. "Curtis, I think it's SO EXCITING about your leg! I mean, about the way you broke it!"

"Oh, yeah?" I said, wondering what kind of crazy story I was going to hear *this* time.

"YES!" exclaimed Mary Jo. "I always wanted to *ride on the back of a fire truck* like that—you know, standing up and holding on? It's too bad you fell off, though. You should have held on tighter when the truck went around the corner."

Pastor Bennett stared at her. "Mary Jo, what *on earth* are you talking about? Only fire fighters can ride on the fire trucks."

Mary Jo shook her head. "No, Daddy, it's true. Curtis got to, didn't you, Curtis?"

Julie added, "That's what some of the kids at school said."

"NO, NO, NO!" I said. I almost jumped up, but I couldn't because of my cast. "Everybody keeps making things up. I just had a little accident, that's all."

"So what happened?" Mary Jo, Julie, and Amy said all together.

I must have had a funny look on my face, because Pastor Bennett squeezed my shoulder. He said, "That's all right, Curtis. When I visit people, some of them want to tell me every detail about their accidents—and some people don't want to talk about what happened at all. So you don't have to tell us if you don't want to."

I was sure glad he said that!

Then Mary Jo noticed the names on my cast, and she wanted to sign her name.

"*Carefully*, Mary Jo!" said Pastor Bennett.

I was glad he said *that*, too! Then he signed his name.

Amy said, "Ju-lee! Show Curtis the cake!"

"Oh!" said Julie. "I was so excited about the fire truck I almost forgot to give this to you."

She carefully took the lid off a plate and showed me a beautiful cake in the shape of a cat. It had white frosting all over it and pink sugar for the inside of the ears. It had gumdrops for the nose and eyes—and skinny licorice for the mouth and whiskers.

"It's beautiful!" I said. "It looks just like your cat Marshmallow."

Julie squirmed a little bit. "Yes. Well,

that's the problem, Curtis. See, this afternoon my mother and I made two cakes. One was going to be for you because of your broken leg and everything. And the other one was going to be for us. I made you a snowman cake. And I made the cat cake for us to eat for dessert. I thought it would be nice, because I like cats."

"You can say that again!" I said. (Julie has *five* cats, God!)

"But Julie yelled at me!" Amy said. "I was going to take a bite out of the ear. And Julie said, 'No, No, No, No! Stop! Stop!' "

Amy laughed her head off, and Julie looked kind of embarrassed. She said, "The problem was, the cake turned out to look *so much* like Marshmallow, I couldn't stand to take a bite out of it. So if you don't mind, could we keep the snowman and give you the cat?"

I said I didn't mind as long as she didn't mind if *I* ate it.

She said, "No, it will be all right. Just don't eat it till I go home, OK?"

"Give him the coconut," said Amy.

Julie reached in her pocket and brought out a plastic bag. The she explained, "The recipe said to put coconut on the cake to make it look fluffy. But I know lots of kids who *hate* coconut. So I thought you could put it on the cake yourself if you like."

Well, it turns out I do like coconut, but I thought it was very smart of Julie to think of that. Julie is always a good thinker. In school Mrs. Whitney puts Julie in charge a lot of times. She puts me in charge, too, but I think it's easy for Julie to be in charge. And I *know* it's hard for me.

"Julie, aren't you going to sign the cast?" Mary Jo said.

Julie purposely wrote small, but she still took up a lot of room. That's because when she saw that Becky had written No-el's name, she thought that was a good idea. So she wrote the names of all her cats: Marshmallow, Setsu, Suki, Sumi, and Oreo.

So what will happen if someone who doesn't know Julie reads my cast? He'll say, "Curtis, you have a friend named *Marshmallow*??"

Amy had to sign her name, too, and she writes big because she's only in kindergarten. So that took up more room. But I think there will still be plenty of room left for the other kids in my class when I go back to school.

● ● ●

I'm in bed now, God, but I get to have the light on for a little while.

My mother thought it would be too hard

for me to get up and down stairs with my crutches. So my parents fixed up a bed for me in the sun-room. This will be my room for as long as I have my cast, but I have to share the space with my mother's plants.

I have a lot of my stuff around me, but it's not the same as being in my own room. It's funny to think of it being empty and dark up there without me.

My mother is staying home with me again tomorrow. I think I can go back to school on Monday. And I sure hope people forget all those crazy stories by then. I don't know how those stories got started in the first place.

Don't get me wrong, God, I think they're interesting stories. They sound like some of the things I make up about that boy called Jamie. So maybe that's what the kids are doing—just making up stories about my broken leg because it's fun to do that. Probably they don't *really* believe that I could do all that stuff. Like playing with teenagers. And saving babies. And riding on fire trucks.

But it feels funny to hear wild stories about an ordinary person. Because one thing's for sure: I'm just an ordinary kid.

So when people tell me crazy stories about the brave way I broke my leg, I'm going to say the stories aren't true.

But another thing's for sure: I'm not going to say how I *really* fell and broke my leg. I'm not telling WHERE or HOW or WHY. And no one can make me.

But it's OK for you to know, God. Because no matter if a person's brave and smart or scared and goofy, you love him anyway. I love you, too, God.

Good night from Curtis.

31

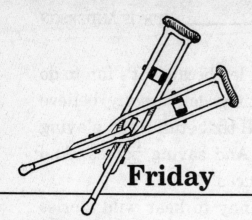

Friday

Dear God,

When I woke up this morning I forgot I had a broken leg. But then I remembered when I tried to get out of bed! The people in my family always tease me because I wake up so groggy in the morning. They all wake up bright and cheerful, but it takes me a long time just to get my eyes open.

I decided it's very frustrating to have a broken leg. At breakfast I started thinking about all the things I won't be able to do when I go back to school. Like, I can't be T.A. (which stands for Teacher's Assistant), because the T.A. has to get up and move around a lot. I can't have gym class and be team leader in the relays. I can't go out at recess and run around and say, "Hey, let's chase somebody!" and have all the boys follow me.

I feel kind of funny about it, God, because I'm sort of *glad* I don't have to do all that stuff. But then I think—will people still like me if I'm not being the leader?

● ● ●

After school Becky, Pug, and Danny all came over at the same time with my work. I am all caught up on the stuff I have to do for Mrs. Whitney, so maybe I can finish the new work tonight.

But Becky had bad news. Mrs. Jones was back today, and—sure enough—she was mad that the kids had acted up for the sub. So Mrs. Jones gave everybody extra work to do over the weekend! How do you like that? Becky got punished with all the other kids, and she never makes a *peep* in class. And I got punished—*and I wasn't even there*!

But anyway. That was the bad news.

The *good* news is that the kids got to sign up today for the P.T.A. Winter Carnival, which is going to be on Saturday, a week from tomorrow. Parents and relatives will buy tickets at the school. And the kids will put on all sorts of contests for people to watch. There will be stuff like a sled race and a snowball-throwing contest. And there will be a snowman-decorating contest to see which team makes the most creative snowman.

Danny said Mrs. Whitney passed around a clipboard with a pencil tied to it by a string. On the clipboard there was a sheet with a list of things to do in the carnival. You had to pick *one* contest to enter and sign your name on the line.

Becky said, "So I signed up for our room's snowman-decorating team. And when Mary Jo and Julie saw my name there, they signed up for that, too."

Pug said, "They needed some boys, so I signed up. But the best part is that Danny is on the team, and he's going to be team leader!"

"Yes, that will work out great," said Becky. "Because Danny draws so well. First he's going to draw some ways the snowman could look. Then we'll all decide which one to do. It's supposed to be creative and everything. We have to come up with a title and write it on a sign. They gave us an example—*The World's Oldest Snowman*. Only we're not allowed to copy

35

that. We have to come up with our own idea."

Pug said, "That's why it's great Danny is team leader. I mean, he's so good in art he even gets to be in Mr. Collins's after-school art club. And that's usually just for the older kids."

All the time Becky and Pug were saying these neat things about him, Danny just sat there, looking kind of shy and proud at the same time. It's like he knew the things they were saying about him were absolutely true, but he didn't want to be the one to say them himself. All he said was, "Mr. Collins cancelled art club next week so kids could practice for the carnival."

If people say good things about you, I think it's better if the things they say are absolutely true. I guess that's the way it is for you, God—more than for anyone else. Because people can say the most excellent, wonderful things about you. And no matter how good those things are, they're always absolutely true.

Anyway, Danny, Pug, Mary Jo, Julie, and Becky will be on the snowman-decorating team from Mrs. Whitney's class. They will be up against five teams from other classes. I hope the team from Mrs. Whitney's class wins!

The contest will be held in the field behind the school where we play baseball in the spring and summer. Each team will have its own spot to work. There's already a lot of snow on the ground, but Danny's hoping we'll get more.

He says each team has to plan its snowman ahead of time and have all the decorations ready in a bag. The kids can ask adults to lend them stuff, but the kids have to do all the planning themselves.

On the day of the Winter Carnival, the teams will get there early to make their snowmen. Then, when it's time for the contest, the teams will all stand behind a line. When the grown-up in charge says, "On your marks, get set, go!" the teams will run to their spots and decorate their snowmen. There's no prize for being the first team done, but they have only FIVE MINUTES to finish. So the teams have to know exactly what they're doing and work *fast!*

Mary Jo and Julie came by to say "Hi" while the other kids were still talking about the Winter Carnival.

"You know," said Julie. "We should make a snowman this week to practice on.

That way, we'll be good and ready for Saturday. We'll have all our stuff in the bag. And we'll know how to decorate the snowman fast."

"Good idea," said Danny. And he wrote it down on a piece of paper: *Practice decorating snowman this week.*

"And here's another thing!" said Mary Jo. She lowered her voice and looked around as if she thought someone might be listening. "We have to find a good *place* to practice. Because—there are *spies everywhere!*

"Spies!" said Danny. "I never thought of that!"

"Oh, yes," said Mary Jo. "I overheard some kids from Mrs. O'Hara's class talking about you being our team leader. They're worried because they think *we'll* have more good ideas than they will. I think

39

they're going to try and find out what we're doing so they can *copy*."

That was such a serious thought that everybody just sat there for a minute without saying a thing. Danny wrote down: *Find good, safe place to practice decorating snowman.*

Finally Becky said, "Well, I know one place that *isn't* good, and that's my apartment building. We don't have a very big yard in back."

"Yes," said Mary Jo. "And there are all those windows that spies could look out of. So Becky's yard is out. And I don't think *my* yard would be very good either, because it's so open."

"And it's right next door to the church," added Julie. "People are always coming and going there. Not to mention just driving by. The corner of Apple Street and

Vine is *so busy*! *My* house would probably work best—*if* we can keep Amy from bothering us."

Pug said, "My little sister, Cindy, wouldn't bother us as much as Amy. The only problem is, this girl from Mrs. O'Hara's class lives next door to me. So she could watch everything we do."

"That's no good," said Danny. "*My* house would be pretty good. At least I don't have any little brothers or sisters running around."

"That's true," said Julie. "But if kids from another team want to find out what we're doing, and if they know you're our team leader, then your house would be the first place they'd look."

Everyone got really quiet again, thinking.

Then suddenly Becky remembered her dog-walking job and jumped up to leave.

Julie said to Becky, "If you wait up, Mary Jo and I will go with you." Then Julie said to Danny, "Let us know when you want to have a meeting of the snowman team, OK?"

"Yes," said Becky. "Tell us if you decide to meet at your house or Julie's."

"And remember!" whispered Mary Jo. "There are *spies everywhere!*"

"Right," said Danny.

After the girls left, Danny said, "Well, I guess I'd better go home and start drawing snowmen."

"I'll come with you," said Pug.

So they said good-bye, and all of a sudden I was by myself again.

It was good everybody came over to see

me, but it feels funny when there's a whole bunch of people in the room with you, and then there's not. I had been by myself except for my mother all day, and it didn't bother me. But now I am feeling kind of lonely, God.

Then I got to thinking about the good news. You know—about the carnival and the snowman team and everything. And all of a sudden I thought to myself, Hey, Curtis. That's not such good news for *you*, is it? *You* didn't get to sign up for any team. Maybe you can go next Saturday to *watch*, but that's *all*. After all, you have a *broken leg*. And it's your *own—dumb—fault!*

I can make myself feel pretty bad when I talk like that, God. I thought I felt bad about my broken leg before, but after I got done talking to myself I felt worse than ever. I felt terrible!

I felt so bad I decided I'd better go do my homework so I wouldn't have to waste a good mood doing it. That is, if I ever get in a good mood again!

Well, love from your sad boy,
Curtis James.

Saturday

Dear God,

I was feeling pretty sad last night, but I'm feeling better this morning.

That's because something extra nice happened today. I got a get-well card from my brother, Coby, at college. It wasn't a letter to the family, like he sends once in a while. It was addressed just to me.

The card is real funny, so I like to look at it a lot. Coby wrote a note at the bottom that said, *Tough break, kid!* He also put *(Ha, Ha)*, so I'd know that *break* was a kind of word-joke. Then he wrote, *Take it easy, Curtis. Don't overdo. Love, Coby.*

46

My parents probably told him that I broke my leg *in the bathroom,* but Coby didn't say anything about that in his card. So I think maybe he's pretending to me that he doesn't know, which is nice. So I'll just pretend to myself that he doesn't know either.

And Coby's card wasn't the only mail I got! There was a get-well card from Miss Jenkins, too.

And then right after I got Miss Jenkins's card, she called me. She talked to my mother first to check something with her. Then Miss Jenkins told me what it was. She said since her Sunday school room is up two flights of stairs, it will be hard for me to get up and down on my crutches. So she's going to see about finding another place for our Sunday school class. But tomorrow, she and the kids are going to meet

47

at Apple Street Church and walk over
here! (Some of the grown-ups at church
have Sunday school in someone's house,
but none of the kids get to.) That was a
nice surprise, God, and I am looking for-
ward to tomorrow.

● ● ●

I got out my reading work that was still
left over from last night. I worked really
hard and finally got it done. Then the
doorbell rang, and I was really glad, because I wanted to think about something
else for a change.

Before I broke my leg, I used to be the
one who always answered the door, because I always got there first. Everyone
would hear the doorbell and think, "Oh,
well. Curtis will get it."

But now it's too much trouble to get up
and get my crutches. Besides, by the time I

could get there, the poor person on the doorstep would probably freeze. So there goes my door-answering job.

My mother answered the door, and it was her friend Mrs. Smith from across the street. The Smiths are moving to another town, and Mrs. Smith brought some of her plants over to give them to my mother. They brought them into the sun-room, which is my room for a while.

The sun-room is nice, because it juts out from the side of our house and has windows on all three sides. I can look out the front to the Smiths' house across the street. And I can look out the side to the ravine beside our house. And I can look out the back to our yard.

"How's the packing coming along?" my mother asked Mrs. Smith.

Mrs. Smith looked up from signing my

cast and said, "Oh, this is going to be the easiest move ever! I'm packing some small things myself, but the Tip-Top Movers are coming Thursday, and they'll do most of the packing and loading for us."

"That will make it so much easier," agreed my mother.

They made room for the new plants and had a snack with me in the sun-room before Mrs. Smith had to go home and clean out closets.

It was nice to see Mrs. Smith, but she is really my mother's friend, and I started wondering what *my* friends were doing. I figured they were building a snowman someplace. I wondered if they went to Julie's house or Danny's.

● ● ●

It's snowing again—those big, fat flakes that I like so much. You know, it's too bad

50

I'm not on the snowman team, God, because my yard would be a good place to practice in. For one thing, I don't have any little brothers and sisters to mess with us. And for another thing, there aren't kids from other classes who live nearby. But best of all, my yard is all kind of closed in and private. Here's a map of it:

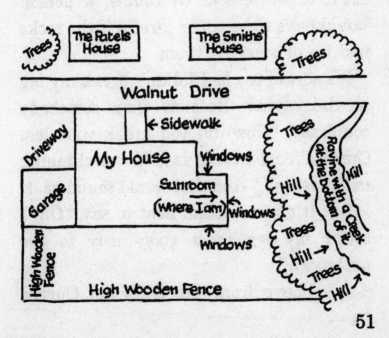

Don't you agree with me, God, that my backyard would be a good place to make a practice snowman?

I wish I could go out and play in my yard right now! I wish I could go play in the ravine. It is a great place for hiding and climbing. There are these nice, big rocks you can use sort of like stairs to go up and down to the creek. Of course, a person would have to be super careful if the rocks had ice or snow on them.

It's sort of too bad I didn't break my leg in the ravine. Because then somebody could say, "How did you break your leg, Curtis?" And I could say, "I was climbing in the ravine." And that would sound neat.

But it *doesn't* sound neat to say, "Oh, I broke my leg *in a goofy way in the bathroom.*"

Love, from your crazy kid, Curtis.

Sunday

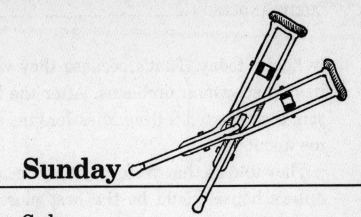

Dear God,

Remember I said Miss Jenkins was going to bring the whole Sunday school class over to my house? Well, that's what she did, and we all sat around my dining room table. It was even better than I thought it was going to be, because Miss Jenkins brought donuts as a special treat. So we were really like the grown-ups' Sunday school class then—only we had juice instead of coffee.

Pug, Danny, Mary Jo, Julie, and Becky all seemed really glad to have Sunday school at my house. But they weren't totally happy today. That's because they were having snowman problems. After the lesson, they started telling Miss Jenkins and me about it.

They told us that yesterday they decided Julie's house would be the best place to work. But—sure enough—Amy kept driving them crazy. So Julie went to her mother's sewing room to complain. And that's when they got the *really* bad news.

Mrs. Chang sews special clothes—like for weddings and things. And when Julie went in her mother's sewing room, she couldn't believe her eyes. There was this *girl from school*, getting fitted for a bridesmaid's dress for her cousin's wedding.

Julie knew her mother was going to have customers that day, but she *didn't* know one of them would be someone from school, someone from *another class*!

54

And the worst part was, Mrs. Chang's sewing room window faces the backyard where the kids were trying to work.

"I don't think that girl, Pam, was there purposely to spy," Julie said. "I mean, I think Pam really *is* going to be in her cousin's wedding. But you never know. Pam's going to be at my house for fittings, and she might tell someone in her class what our team is doing."

"Did she see your snowman decorations?" I asked.

"No," said Julie. "Danny hasn't finished the drawings yet. He's kind of being a perfectionist. I ought to know because that's what Mrs. Whitney says I am. Anyway, we just wanted to practice building the plain snowman first. But we couldn't even get the snowman built because of *Amy*. And my mother didn't even do anything about

55

that, because she couldn't understand why we wouldn't let Amy play with us."

Mary Jo said, "It's not like we *never* let Amy play with us! Besides, the snowman isn't regular playing. It's *serious!*"

Danny sighed. "I think we're going to have to work at my house after all," he said. "At least there are no little kids around."

"I think you're right," said Pug. "We can take turns being the lookout to make sure no one's watching us."

"The only trouble with that," said Becky, "is that *all five* people should be practicing on the snowman at the same time. It won't be like the real team if only four of us are working at a time."

All of them agreed that she was right, but they didn't know what else to do.

Just listening to them talk about the

snowman—even about the snowman *prob-lem*—made me feel lonely in a funny kind of way. Everybody was being very nice to me. And they were even having Sunday school at my house. But they were on the snowman team, having all these problems together, and I wasn't.

• • •

Mary Jo, Becky, and Julie walked back to church with Miss Jenkins. But Pug and Danny rode with my parents and me.

I had some trouble getting out of the house and into the car, but we worked it out OK. I thought, this is good practice for going to school tomorrow. After all, someone is going to have to drive me and pick me up for weeks!

And another way church was good practice for school was getting over all the fuss people made of me.

Lots of people asked me what happened, but all I would say was that I fell. Whew!

● ● ●

After dinner, I went out to my sun-room-bedroom to rest a little bit. And that's when I got my GREAT IDEA!!!

I called Danny and told him to come over right away, because I had something important to ask him.

"What's up!" asked Danny as I led him into the sun-room.

"Look at my backyard!" I said. "It's got two high fences and a ravine. It's all kind of closed in and private."

"Yes," Danny said slowly, like he couldn't figure out why I was telling him this.

"Don't you *see*?" I asked. "My yard would be a *perfect place* for you to build a practice snowman! I don't have any little brothers or sisters to bother us. And the spies might not even think of looking for us here, because they wouldn't even know I was on the team."

"But how can you be on the team with a broken leg?" Danny asked.

"Well, maybe I couldn't go out there and help you build exactly," I said. "But I could sit in the sun-room here and keep watch— just in case. That way you could all work on the snowman at the same time."

Then I showed Danny how if I looked out the front windows I could see the Smiths' house across the street with the SOLD sign in the yard. And if I looked out the side I could see the ravine. And if I looked out the back I could see the backyard.

"See?" I said. "I could be on the team as lookout. You could all meet at my house. It would be perfect!"

59

But Danny didn't jump up and down and get all excited the way I thought he would. Instead he just stared at his shoe and said, "I don't want to do it that way."

I don't mind telling you, God, I was really surprised when Danny said that! I mean, when a person gets a GREAT IDEA, it seems like other people should think it's at least a *good* idea.

"Why don't you want to do it that way?" I asked him.

"Because," he answered.

"Because why?"

"Just because."

"Just because why?"

Danny was quiet for a while. Finally he said, "Because you get picked for stuff all the time, Curtis. You always get to be in charge. If we meet at your house, it will be like *you're* in charge of the snowman team from Mrs. Whitney's room."

"But I'll only be the lookout," I said.

"It doesn't matter," said Danny. "You always get lots of attention. People are used to you always being the leader. If you come on the team, people might forget that *I'm* supposed to be the leader."

"No, they won't," I said.

"They might," said Danny. "I don't get picked for stuff that much. I'm not a superkid like you."

"I'm not a superkid!" I said. "I'm just a regular person who would make a good lookout for people who need one. And my yard is just a good place to practice, that's all. You don't want spies copying your ideas, do you?"

Danny just shook his head.

"Then please say I can be on the team as yard owner and lookout! OK?"

"I don't know," said Danny. "I'll think about it for a while, all right?"

"All right," I said. I figured it wouldn't do any good to keep asking him right then.

● ● ●

It's later now, God, and I have to go to sleep so I can get up for school tomorrow. But I'm having trouble getting to sleep, because I keep thinking about what Danny said.

I don't like it that he thinks I'm a superkid, because I'm not, not, not, NOT. Maybe I should have told him how and where I broke my leg. *Then* he sure wouldn't call me *superkid*!

Besides, I think it's *perfect* that Danny is team leader, because he is so good in art, and the snowman is supposed to be creative. I don't *want* to be the leader. All I want is to be on the team. So maybe Danny will think it over and let me.

Tomorrow I'm just going to be real quiet and take it easy at school so that Danny can see what a regular kid I am. The class will probably make a fuss about my broken leg and want to sign my cast and everything. But after that, everything will be so ordinary you won't believe it.

So good night and love from your regular, ordinary boy, Curtis.

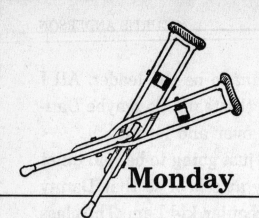

Monday

Dear God,

This was supposed to be a nice, regular, ordinary, unsuper day, right? But, as you know, that's not how it worked out. So I will just write about it from the beginning, OK?

• • •

It all started when my mother made me go in late to school because she and Mrs. Whitney didn't want me trying to get through the crowded halls on my crutches.

My mother drove me, and we went in the back way, through the teachers' parking lot. It was dark and cloudy this morning, and I noticed one of the cars still had its lights on. My dad left his lights on once, and his battery got so worn down the car wouldn't start. So I stopped at the office and told Mrs. Miller, the secretary.

● ● ●

When I got to my class in Room 110, everybody looked up at the same exact minute, and they all made the same funny kind of gasping noise. (You'd think they never saw a cast before in their whole lives!)

Mrs. Whitney picked this boy named Peter to help me with the stuff I couldn't do by myself. Like, he helped me take my knapsack off and put it on the floor. Then he helped me sit at my desk. I had to bring a pillow from home to put on a chair, so I could have my leg up. And Peter helped me with that, too.

65

He seemed really glad that Mrs. Whitney had picked him. And all the time he was helping me I thought: I bet if someone else had a broken leg instead of me, Mrs. Whitney would have picked me to be the helper. (Unless it was a girl, and then she would have picked Julie.) And I wondered if maybe Mrs. Whitney automatically picks the same people too much, and if that bothers the other kids—like Peter or Pug or Danny.

I saw Danny watching me, and I knew he thought I was getting a lot of attention. But the attention was just because of my broken leg, so I thought that things would get ordinary right away.

● ● ●

But right after that, Mr. Harley, the principal, got on the intercom to make announcements. For one thing, he told us Mr.

Beck, the superintendent of schools, was there to spend the whole day at our school. That was all right, but then he said, "Mr. Beck would like to extend his personal thanks to the student who noticed and reported that a car still had its lights on. That was Mr. Beck's car, and I understand that Curtis Anderson was the student who reported it. Good work, Curtis! You rescued that battery!"

Everyone turned to stare at me again. But the one I wondered about was Danny. So I kind of peeked at him out of the corner of my eye. He was looking at me and shaking his head a little bit as if he were thinking, "What will superkid do next?"

I was going to talk to him privately about letting me be on the snowman team, but I figured I should let things settle down and get ordinary first.

Of course, Mrs. Whitney asked me how I broke my leg, but I was ready. I said real politely, "I just fell is all. That's all I can say." Then I secretly clamped down on my teeth so that nothing could accidentally slip out about falling *in the bathroom* or about how—well, you know.

Mrs. Whitney let the kids line up, a few at a time, to sign my cast, and she told them not to dawdle. I think she wanted to have a regular, ordinary day, too.

The kids were whispering, but no one asked me any more about my leg, which made me wonder what was going on.

Peter was the last one to sign my cast, and I asked him what people were whispering about.

He said, "Don't worry, Curtis. We all understand why you can't talk about what happened to your leg."

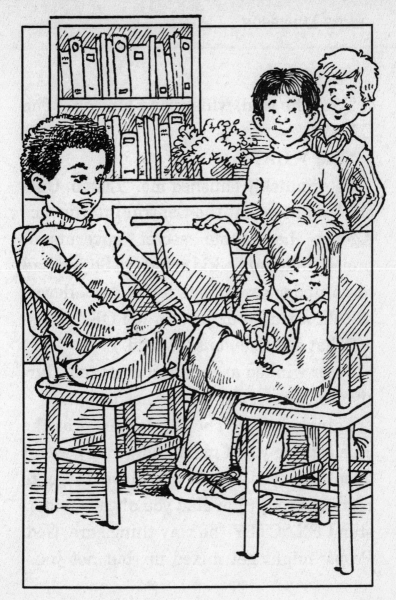

"You *do*?"

"Yes!" he said, whispering himself. "The C.I.A."

"The WHAT?"

Peter quickly shushed me. "Listen, Curtis. We know that the Central Intelligence Agency had some secret government project that only a kid could do. So you had to go under cover, and you're not allowed to talk about your job. So it's OK."

"That is *ridiculous!*" I said.

Peter winked at me. "I understand, Curtis. You can count on me not to tell."

I give up, God! The C.I.A. story was the craziest one yet! I mean, how many secret agents do you know who have to go to reading group? I'm glad you always understand EXACTLY the way things are, God. *People* might get mixed up, but not *you*.

● ● ●

Reading turned out to be a nice surprise. That's because Mrs. Jones got a new student teacher today, and she will be taking our reading group. We met in the downstairs library so that I wouldn't have to try to get upstairs on my crutches. For reading, Becky took over from Peter as my helper. She carried my books and pillow and walked extra slowly so I could keep up.

I felt so good about Miss Duncan, the student teacher, and not having to worry about the stairs that I thought sure the rest of the day would go OK.

● ● ●

When Becky and I got back, Mrs. Whitney was setting up the filmstrip projector. I knew I wouldn't have any jobs to do because of my leg. So I just sat there and looked around. I was hoping Danny would notice how ordinary I was being. I thought I would ask him at lunch what he decided about using my yard.

But while I was looking around, I noticed that the hook for the movie screen above the chalkboard was coming loose. And I noticed it right at the same minute Mrs. Whitney went to pull the screen down. So I yelled, "Mrs. Whitney! Look out!"

She jumped back in time, but I guess she must have jiggled the screen, because the whole thing came crashing down.

Everything was absolutely silent for a second. And then Mary Jo jumped up and hollered, "CURTIS! YOU SAVED THE TEACHER'S LIFE!!!"

That was the very minute Mrs. O'Hara from next door came rushing in because of the crash. She is kind of nervous anyway, God, so when she heard what Mary Jo was saying, she just about fainted.

Mrs. Whitney made Mrs. O'Hara sit down and take deep breaths. And Mrs. Whitney kept saying over and over, "No, I don't need an ambulance. I'm fine. The kids are fine. *Everything's* fine!"

Of course, Mary Jo was exaggerating—she does that a lot. But the kids—especially the boys—acted kind of funny about the whole thing. Some of the boys slapped me on the back and said, "Way to go, Curtis!" But some of the other boys grumbled because *they* weren't the ones who noticed the hook was loose.

Danny is my friend, so he tried to look happy for me, but I think he really felt like grumbling. I decided I'd wait till afternoon recess to talk to him about how I didn't want to be the team leader, just the lookout.

● ● ●

Mrs. Whitney had something special planned for the afternoon.

At the beginning of winter, she taught us this neat poem. I will copy it here, God:

First Snow
by Marie Louise Allen
Snow makes whiteness where it falls.
The bushes look like popcorn balls.
The places where I always play
Look like somewhere else today.

Mrs. Whitney said because we had so much snow lately, and because the Winter Carnival was coming up, we could make popcorn balls.

74

A couple of mothers came in to help, and we all went down to the school kitchen.

The kids had to stand, but I had to sit on the kitchen stool with my leg propped up on a chair. I was just sitting there quietly, beside the stove.

Well, I don't know how it happened exactly, but a little drop of cooking oil spilled on the burner and flared up. That happened to my mother one time, and she dumped baking soda on the fire to put it out. Mrs. Whitney had a box of baking soda handy on the counter, so I grabbed it and shook a bunch of soda on the flame. It put the fire right out.

Everything was absolutely silent for a second. Then Mary Jo whirled around and yelled, "CURTIS! YOU KEPT THE SCHOOL FROM BURNING DOWN!!!"

She was exaggerating. But I figured I wouldn't try to talk to Danny after all.

So that's how the day went, God. Let's see. I rescued the superintendent's car. I saved Mrs. Whitney's life. I kept the school from burning down. And everyone thinks I work for the C.I.A.

This was not a very good day.

So good night and love from Curtis, who everyone thinks is a superkid.

But he's not.

Tuesday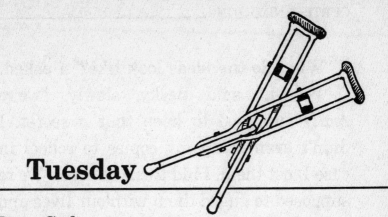

Dear God,

All the other kids are out running around at recess. But, of course, I have to stay inside because of my leg. So this is a good time to write in my prayer journal.

Becky told me on the way to reading group that the team went over to Danny's house yesterday to look at his snowman drawings, which he decided were *finally* ready for people to see. He even made copies for each person on the team. Danny came up with three ideas. Becky said the kids are supposed to think about which one they want to do.

"What do the ideas look like?" I asked.

"Wel-l-l," said Becky, slowly, "we're *really* supposed to keep that a secret. I didn't even bring my copies to school in case I lost them. I hid them at home. We're supposed to guard them with our lives and not tell *anyone*."

That made sense. But I felt that funny kind of loneliness again.

Becky said, "Most of us have stuff we have to do today. So we're going to start building the snowman at Danny's house tomorrow."

"What about spies?" I asked.

Becky shrugged. "We're still worried about them, so I guess we'll have to take turns being the lookout."

So there you have it, God. It doesn't seem like Danny has changed his mind about letting me be the team lookout and

78

using my yard for practices. But I figure if I have a very good, unsuper day, Danny might change his mind after all.

● ● ●

It is after supper now. And this turned out to be a very good day, God. Nothing special happened at all!

But then—guess what happened just now! Danny called me!

He said, "So, do you still want to be on the snowman team or what?"

"Sure!" I said. "What made you change your mind?"

"Well," Danny said, "I figured maybe some of the neat stuff you did yesterday might have been by accident. Maybe you don't want to be team leader after all."

"That's what I've been telling you all along!!" I said happily.

"But I have to talk to you." Danny

79

sounded very serious and worried. "The snowman team has a BIG PROBLEM. My aunt and uncle both have the flu."

I shook the phone because I thought maybe some of Danny's words were getting lost. I was sorry to hear his relatives were sick, but what did that have to do with building a snowman? So I asked Danny that.

And he answered in one word: *"Triplets."*

"Oh, no!" I cried. "You mean your *cousins* are staying with you again?"

"You got it," said Danny. "My mother just left to pick them up. There's *no way* we can get anything done with three, little, preschool, triplet girls running around! So the team will come over to your house after school tomorrow, OK?"

I couldn't believe my ears, God! It was WONDERFUL, STUPENDOUS, EX-

CITING, FABULOUS, TERRIFIC, SPEC-
TACULAR, MARVELOUS!!!

"OK," I said to Danny. "Talk to you
tomorrow."

So I'll say good night to you, too, God.
With love from regular, ordinary Curtis,
who wants you to know that he isn't
really glad that Danny's aunt and uncle
are sick, even if it might seem like it.

Wednesday

Dear God,

This morning Danny told Mrs. Whitney that my name should be on the snowman team list, too. Then after school the snowman team came over to my house to practice. But they figured it would be too obvious to any spies who might be watching if all of them came over at the same time. So they each came separately. And they tried to take the most complicated routes they could think of to throw off anyone who might be following.

Becky got there first. She said her brother Bobby was doing her dog-walking job for her so that she could come to snowman practice. But she brought No-el with her. That way, any spy who saw her would think she was just some kid out walking a puppy.

Anyway, it took everyone a long time to get here. When they finally did, they all got out their copies of the snowman sketches Danny had made. Danny even had some new copies he made just for me—which was *very nice* of him, God. So even though I couldn't go outside, I still felt like I really belonged on the snowman team.

Here are the snowman ideas Danny came up with:

We all thought that The New Year Snowbaby was the most creative. So that made it unanimous. (We thought it would be so neat to put a diaper on a snowman!! Who else would think of that?)

← Party Hat

Stick

Stick

Happy New Year

Banner

Diaper (old sheet)

THE NEW YEAR SNOWBABY

← Wig

← Glasses

Stick

← Earring

Big Shiny Buttons

Stick

Pointer

Stick

Skirt (old tablecloth)

THE TEACHER SNOWLADY

← Straw Hat

Sunglasses

Hawaiian Shirt

Stick

Suntan Lotion

Bathing Suit (old pants)

THE BEACHCOMBER SNOWMAN

Becky, Julie, and Mary Jo thought the second most creative was The Teacher Snowlady. And they thought the third most creative was The Beachcomber Snowman.

But Danny, Pug, and I thought just the opposite. We thought The Beachcomber Snowman was the second most creative and The Teacher Snowlady was the third most creative.

We argued about it for a while until Julie said it really didn't matter, because we all agreed on the *first* most creative, and we were wasting time. Well, we couldn't argue with that!

We decided that this afternoon the kids would go outside and make the snowman in my backyard while I kept a lookout from the sun-room. Then tonight we would all collect stuff for the decorations. And tomorrow the kids would come back over here to practice putting the decorations on.

So the kids went out in the yard, and I went into the sun-room with No-el. Becky thought No-el would get in the way of the snowman almost as much as Amy or the triplets. No-el isn't a newborn puppy. But Becky said even if you figure by dog's age, he is still just a preschooler.

Before Danny went outside with the others, he turned back and said to me, "Probably there won't be any spies by your house, but keep a good lookout anyway. If we know the spies haven't found out we're working in your yard, it'll be safe to put the decorations on tomorrow."

I promised to do my super-extra-*extra* best. Danny said being an ordinary lookout was good enough as long as I kept the spies away.

I figured out a good lookout system. Part of the time I looked out the back windows at the kids making the snowman. Pug, Danny, and Mary Jo started rolling the large, bottom snowball from one direction. And Julie and Becky started rolling the smaller snowball from the opposite direction.

Then part of the time I looked out the side windows and checked the ravine.

And part of the time I looked out the front windows to make sure no spies were going by on the street.

It was when I was looking out the front windows that something started feeling funny to me. I started thinking so hard about it that I forgot about the snowman out back. I forgot about the ravine at the side. I just kept watching out the front windows.

What I saw were movers at the Smiths' house. They were carrying out furniture and stuff and loading it into a van that said "Quik-Go Movers."

Then suddenly I remembered Mrs. Smith saying, "Oh, this is going to be the easiest move ever. . . . The Tip-Top Movers are coming Thursday."

"Something's wrong here," I said to Noel. "That van says 'Quik-Go Movers,' and it's not Thursday yet. It's only Wednesday. I wonder if the Smiths changed their minds?"

I didn't see the Smiths anywhere. Their car wasn't in the driveway. It didn't even look as if they were home. I thought for sure they'd want to be there when the movers came!

"Mom!" I called. "Come here a minute!" Then I remembered that my mother was out grocery shopping and that my father and Claudia weren't home yet.

I went to the back door and called the kids as quietly as I could. They all came rushing in, stamping the snow off their boots and all talking at once. "What's the matter? Spies? What's wrong?"

"Shhh!" I said. "No, not spies. But something funny's going on!"

They followed me into the sun-room. I told them to duck down so no one would see them peeking out the windows. I explained about the Smiths. And I said, "I think maybe those people aren't the movers at all. I think maybe they're burglars."

"Oh, boy!" said Mary Jo. "Let's go chase them away."

"Are you crazy?" asked Pug.

"No," said Mary Jo. "We could take Noel with us for protection."

"Mary Jo, be reasonable!" said Julie. "Curtis, did you tell your mom?"

"She's not home!" I said, feeling really nervous, because I knew I'd better do something FAST. I swallowed hard. "I'm going to call the police," I said.

"Wow!" said Becky. "I've never called the police before!"

My hand was shaking as I pushed the telephone buttons for the police emergency number. I explained why I was calling.

I was afraid the police would think I was just some kid fooling around. I mean, I may be goofy, but I'd never do anything *that* dumb! But I guess the police could tell I was serious.

"What did they say?" Julie asked when I hung up.

"They said they'd send a police car over right away," I said.

"So what do we do now?" asked Mary Jo.

I shrugged, trying not to look as scared as I felt. "I guess all we can do is wait."

So we crouched down by the windows and kept our eyes on the moving van. My heart was pounding so hard I could hardly stand it.

Suddenly No-el made a low, growling noise in his throat.

"What's the matter?" whispered Mary Jo. Her voice was shaking.

"No-el hears something!" Becky whispered back. Her voice was shaking, too.

Then we all heard the door from my garage open. No-el jumped up and charged out of the room, barking his head off.

That's when we all started screaming. And that's when my mother rushed in with a bag of groceries in her arms. No-el ran along beside her, wagging his tail.

When we saw it was my mother, we all just collapsed. It took her awhile to get the whole story, because we were all talking at once. And we couldn't stop chattering no matter how hard we tried.

But at last she understood. And it felt *so good* now that she was in charge. With my mother there, it was actually fun waiting to see what would happen.

● ● ●

Well, as you know, God, my hunch was right—the "Quik-Go Movers" were PHONIES.

They knew the Smiths were moving, and they found a way to get them out of town—some phone call about a problem with their new house, I think. Then the burglars brought their own truck, decorated to look like a moving van. They cleaned out the house. They thought no one would notice a moving van at a house where the people were going to be moving.

But the police got there just in time and caught them. The Smiths came home early because they were afraid something was up, and they made a big fuss over me.

Danny said to me privately, "OK, maybe you just *happened* to see the superintendent's car lights on. Maybe you just *happened* to see the loose hook and warn Mrs. Whitney. Maybe you just *happened* to be the one closest to the baking soda. But now you just *happened* to stop a burglary?? If that's not being a superkid, Curtis, I don't know what is!"

"Does that mean I can't be on the team anymore?" I asked, feeling really worried.

Danny thought for a minute. "You can stay. We really need you as a lookout. But everything you do is so special. It's not

94

fair, Curtis! I mean, if *I* broke *my* leg, it would probably be in the *bathroom* or some dumb thing!"

I opened my mouth to tell Danny that's exactly where I *did* break *my* leg. But the right minute went flying past, and I didn't get my words together fast enough.

So it's been quite a day, God. And tomorrow will be another big day. We're all supposed to collect stuff for The New Year Snowbaby tonight. Then tomorrow the team will practice putting it together.

Good night and love from
Curtis-the-Lookout.

Thursday

Dear God,

There's a teachers' meeting this afternoon, so kids don't have school.

The team is coming over to my house for lunch, and then we're going to practice. My mom took some time off to be with us. I guess she thought if burglars could come when she was grocery shopping, the world might end if she went to work and left me alone the whole afternoon.

● ● ●

"Did you see any spies around here after we left?" Mary Jo asked me.

"No," I said.

"OK," said Danny. "Then it's safe to go out and practice putting on the decorations." He showed us the sign he printed last night that said The New Year Snowbaby. We got out all the stuff we had gathered and put it in a pile. Then my mother gave us a shopping bag for it. The kids put on their coats and boots and went outside. I put on my coat, too, but I just went into the sun-room.

The reason I had to wear a coat was that I was in charge of standing by the open window and yelling, "On your marks. Get set. Go!" (Last night I asked my father if I could use his stopwatch to time the kids. I had to make sure they could do the snowman in five minutes or less.)

The kids drew a line in the snow at the other end of the yard and stood behind it. When I gave them the signal, they ran to the snowman and put on the decorations. The snowman ended up looking really good. But the kids took too long to put it together, because they got into an argument about who was going to do what.

So Danny made each person pick something to do and stick with it. Then they took all the stuff off, put it in the bag, and went back to the starting line.

"On your marks. Get set. Go!" I yelled again. They did better this time, but it still wasn't fast enough.

"One more time," Danny said in his best team-leader voice.

And this time, they did it—even without Becky, who had to leave early to do her dog-walking job.

Julie said, "I think we should try it again tomorrow—just to be SUPER sure."

Everyone agreed with her. They knew

they needed to practice some more, but they had had enough for one day! They took the decorations off the snowman, put them in the shopping bag, and left the bag with me in the sun-room. Everyone went away happy.

I was feeling pretty good myself. I was just taking off my coat when I looked into the ravine and saw a flash of something red. A scarf? A hat? Whatever it was disappeared behind the rocks.

I felt as if someone had punched me in the stomach. I sat down hard on the edge of my bed. *Spies!* I had been so busy timing the kids and yelling, "On your marks, get set, go!" that I had completely forgotten to do my lookout job. *How goofy can you get?*

And yesterday I had been keeping a lookout all right—but out the front of the house at the Smiths' burglars. What if spies had been hiding that whole time in the ravine?

The first thing I wanted to do, of course, was go climbing in the ravine to see if I could catch anyone or find any proof. But I couldn't do anything because of my leg. I felt so frustrated I wanted to scream.

That's when I happened to look out the front windows and see Becky going by on her dog-walking job.

I didn't even stop to worry about what she would think when I told her what happened. I just opened the window and called to her to come quick.

● ● ●

Becky left No-el and Patches with me since she couldn't hold onto them in the ravine. But she took Fifi, the poodle, with her because Becky thinks Fifi is a pretty good detective-dog.

101

I could hardly breathe as I watched Becky and Fifi scrambling around looking for clues. I hoped she wouldn't find anything and that the flash of red had just been my imagination. But I could tell by her face when she came back that the news was NOT GOOD.

"First of all," said Becky, "I found lots of footprints and handprints in the snow. The spies must have crouched down behind the rocks and watched us. I tried it myself, and you can see the snowman just fine from there."

I groaned.

Becky went on. "And second, I found this little bit of red fuzz snagged on a branch. Maybe it came from a hat or scarf or mitten."

"That must have been the flash of red I saw just now," I said. "Someone's hat, scarf, or mitten. But maybe it wasn't spies. Maybe it was just some kids playing."

Becky shook her head. "I don't think so. Because look what else I found."

She had saved her best clue for last. It was a torn piece of yellow-orange paper. I knew right away what it was. Yesterday the teachers all passed out notes from the office reminding the parents that Thursday (today) was going to be a half day.

"And look," said Becky. "The teacher's name was on the part that got torn off, but you can still see the room number."

I read *Room 112* and felt a little sick. That's because Mrs. Whitney's class is *Room 110*. Room 112 is next door to us—Mrs. O'Hara's room. And the kids Mary Jo heard talking about spying on us were from Mrs. O'Hara's room.

"This is *worse* than terrible!" I said.

103

"Those kids were probably here yesterday. And then they came back today to spy on our decorating."

"We'd better tell Danny," Becky said.

"I'll tell him," I said. "But don't tell anyone else for now, OK?"

"OK," said Becky. Then we just both stood around, feeling terrible. We couldn't think of anything to say. Then at last Becky said, "Well, I'd better get going. Fifi's owner gets upset if I'm late getting back from the walk. Let me know what Danny says we should do."

I promised her I would.

● ● ●

I meant to call Danny right then. I really did, God. But I figured I should try and calm down a little bit first.

Then before I knew it, it was time for supper. My dad doesn't like it when people call at suppertime, and I thought maybe Danny's father wouldn't like that either. So I waited.

Then I watched some TV to kind of take my mind off things.

And then it was time for bed.

                    So this is good night
                    and love from Curtis—
who still hasn't called Danny yet.

Friday

Dear God,

It's after school now, and the kids should be here any minute.

First thing this morning Becky asked me if I had talked to Danny. I told her I would do it today. She didn't tell the other kids what she knew about the spies in the ravine. But all day long she kept watching me, like she thought I should tell someone soon.

Except I didn't.

I *meant* to, but the right minute just never came.

All the kids were in a good mood when they came over, because practice had gone so well yesterday.

"OK, team!" Danny said. "Let's go out there and put that New Year Snowbaby together again in record time!"

Becky stared at me really hard.

"Um," I said. "Um. I—I think I'd better tell you guys something. . . ."

● ● ●

Everybody was so shocked that the spies found out about the Snowbaby idea, that they just sat there without saying a word. I wondered if they were trying to decide how to kill me.

"I'm sorry," I said. "I really messed up as a lookout. If I had spotted the spies on Wednesday, or even soon enough yesterday, you wouldn't have gone ahead with

The New Year Snowbaby decorating. But now those kids from Mrs. O'Hara's room know what we're doing. And I should have told you sooner, so you could decide what to do! I *really messed up!*"

Danny said, "I know. I can't believe it!"

Something about the way he said it sounded funny. I looked up quickly and saw that Danny was smiling at me, almost laughing.

He said, "I can't believe how you messed up, Curtis. And I can't believe you were scared to tell us. But don't worry about it. You're *only human.*"

"Thanks!" I said. And I meant it.

Then the other kids all copied Danny and told me not to feel too bad.

The only problem was—what we were going to do for a snowman?

Pug and I thought we should do The

Beachcomber Snowman. Becky, Julie, and Mary Jo wanted to do The Teacher Snowlady. We all got into a kind of fight about it.

But Danny said, "The problem is, those aren't our best ideas! We lost our best idea. If only we could come up with something better."

"Too bad we don't have a robot-computer," I said. "We could just program *him* to come up with something."

"That's it!" Danny yelled. He jumped up, and his eyes were shining. "A robot! We'll make a *robot* snowman! Curtis, do you have some drawing paper?"

I hurried as fast as I could to get it, and the other kids all started talking at once.

As soon as I gave him a pencil and paper, Danny started sketching. "See?" he said. "First of all, we'll make the snowballs kind of square. Now. What can we use for decorations?"

"I have an idea for the nose!" said Mary Jo. "You know that door at the side of the church? Well, it has a yellow night-light over it. I'll ask if I can borrow a yellow light bulb."

"Good idea!" said Danny. He drew a light bulb nose. "And I think I can get some almost-used-up batteries at home. Those will make good eyes for a robot."

"What about a mouth?" asked Pug. "A robot talks like a recording."

"How about a cassette tape?" I said. I went to beg and plead with Claudia to find an old one she didn't want anymore. Then when I told her it had to be a dark one to show up against the snow, she said I was really pushing my luck. But she helped out. So now it will probably be, *Curtis's*

110

Snowman. The Movie. Starring—CLAU-DIA ANDERSON!!!

When I came back to the living room with the tape, The Robot Snowman diagram was just about done. Becky was going to bring her Slinky and borrow Bobby's to make the arms. Danny told her to tie each Slinky to a stick so that she could put them on the snowman real fast tomorrow.

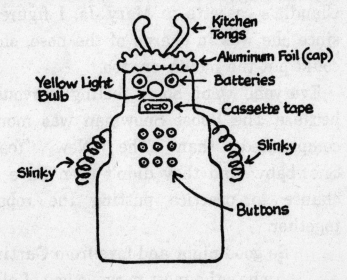

Julie thought of making a panel on the robot's chest with buttons. Pug thought of using kitchen tongs for antennas and aluminum foil for a cap.

"OK," said Danny. "I'll make a new title sign tonight. Everybody bring your stuff to the carnival tomorrow. Whatever you do, don't forget!" He made everybody write down what they were in charge of. I gave Claudia's cassette to Mary Jo. I figured since she was in charge of the nose, she could put the mouth on, too.

Everyone went home feeling nervous, because The Robot Snowman was more complicated than The New Year Snowbaby. And they didn't even have a chance to practice putting the robot together.

So good night and love from Curtis, who's the most nervous one of all.

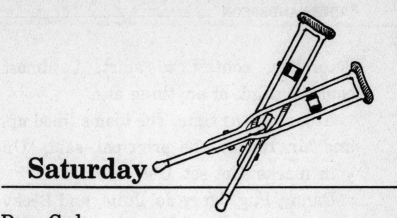

Saturday

Dear God,

My dad drove me over early for the Winter Carnival. I wanted to watch the kids making their snowman, even though I couldn't help them.

But Danny gave me a job to do. He put me in charge of holding the shopping bag full of all the robot stuff.

I thought it was really nice of him to trust me after the way I messed up. Believe me, I guarded that bag with my life!

The Winter Carnival was really neat—with the contests and everything. But I was so nervous waiting for the snowman-decorating contest to start, I almost couldn't think of anything else.

At last it was time. The teams lined up, and Mr. Harley, the principal, said, "On your marks. Get set. Go!"

Danny, Pug, Mary Jo, Julie, and Becky raced to their snowman. Mary Jo was carrying the bag, because the others knew she would get there first.

"Come on, come on, come on," I said under my breath as they worked. "Oh, hurry, hurry!"

We were all seeing The Robot Snowman come together for the first time, and it was like magic. I mean, it looked good on paper. But it looked FANTASTIC, STUPENDOUS, MAGNIFICENT in real life!!!

The judges must have thought so, too, because we finished in time. And we won *first place.*

Mrs. O'Hara's kids came in second, and Guess What They Made: A New Year Snowbaby. We were *furious*! But we decided that hitting those kids or grabbing their second-prize ribbon or wrecking their snowman wouldn't be the best thing to do.

Since Danny was team leader, we decided he should tell Mrs. Whitney about the other kids cheating. But we all went with him in case he forgot anything.

Mrs. Whitney told us just to enjoy our prize and she would take care of the cheating problem. So we all went home with Danny to enjoy our prize by having a party.

● ● ●

When Claudia came to pick me up, I started whining, because I was having a good time and I didn't want to leave yet.

Claudia got really impatient with me,

115

and she said, "Oh, honestly, Curtis James! Do you think it's *fun* driving you and your broken leg around? I should have left you to die in the *bathroom!*"

"Bathroom?" said Danny. "What do you mean—*bathroom*?"

Claudia gulped. Right away she realized that she had accidentally broken her promise not to tell anyone where I was when I fell.

I thought about closing my mouth up tight and not saying any more, but to tell you the truth, God, I was kind of glad finally to tell what really happened.

"I fell in the bathroom," I said. "That's where I was when I broke my leg."

I looked at the kids. I think they were trying hard not to laugh, but they couldn't help it.

"*How*?" asked Pug, trying to keep a

116

straight face. "Did you slip on some soap or something?"

Before I could answer, Claudia the Loyal One jumped right in. "Yeah, Curtis, just how *did* you do it? I never heard the details."

I took a deep breath. I felt like I was going to laugh myself.

"Um. I tried to step from the top . . . of the toilet tank . . . onto the sink. I missed. And that's how I fell."

All those eyes just stared at me. Claudia said very slowly and carefully, "Why— were—you—doing—THAT?"

I answered her, but I must have mumbled, because everyone said, "What? Speak up. We can't hear you."

So I spoke up. "I was playing . . . Mountain Climber. . . . The bathroom is all white, you know? And it sort of looks like a mountain with snow on top. . . ."

I stopped talking. They were all laughing too hard to hear me anyway. I didn't have my stopwatch with me, but I think they laughed for seventeen minutes.

Then the other kids made Claudia leave, so they could tell about the crazy things *they* had done. We all promised we would never tell other people about all this craziness. We would have snowman team secrets. And of all the crazy things, the kids said the way I broke my leg was the craziest.

"Oh, Curtis!" they said, wiping the tears from their eyes. (We were laughing so hard we cried.) "Oh, Curtis! You are One Goofy Kid!"

"Hey, yeah!" I said. "Hey, I guess I am!"
Love from Curtis.

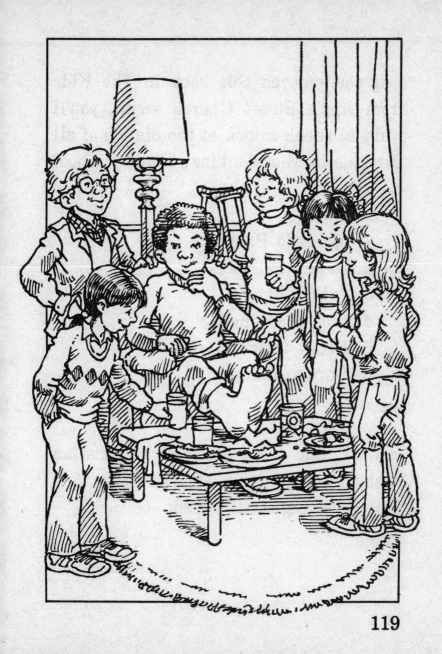

If you enjoyed this book in The Kids from Apple Street Church series, you'll want to sneak a look at the diaries of all the kids in Miss Jenkins's Sunday school class.

1. Mary Jo Bennett
2. Danny Petrowski
3. Julie Chang
4. Pug McConnell
5. Becky Garcia
6. Curtis Anderson

You'll find these books at a Christian bookstore. Or write to Chariot Books, 850 N. Grove, Elgin, IL 60120.